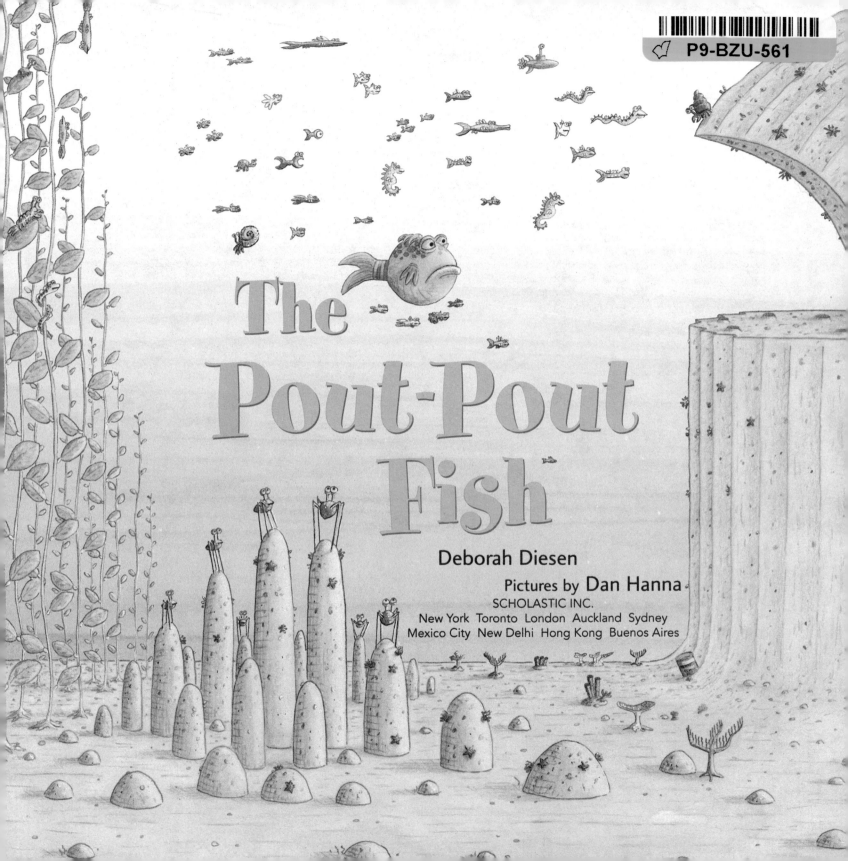

The Pout-Pout Fish

Deborah Diesen

Pictures by **Dan Hanna**

SCHOLASTIC INC.
New York Toronto London Auckland Sydney
Mexico City New Delhi Hong Kong Buenos Aires

For Mason and Isaac
—D.D.

For Stella
—D.H.

ISBN-13: 978-0-545-15562-5
ISBN-10: 0-545-15562-2

Text copyright © 2008 by Deborah Diesen.
Pictures copyright © 2008 by Dan Hanna.
All rights reserved. Published by Scholastic Inc.,
557 Broadway, New York, NY 10012, by arrangement
with Farrar, Straus and Giroux, Inc. SCHOLASTIC and
associated logos are trademarks and/or registered
trademarks of Scholastic Inc.

30   18 19 20/0

Printed in the U.S.A.   40

First Scholastic printing, February 2009

Designed by Jay Colvin

Deep in the water
Where the fish hang out
Lives a glum gloomy swimmer
With an ever-present pout.

"I'm a *pout-pout* fish
With a *pout-pout* face,
So I spread the dreary-wearies
All over the place."

BLUB

BLUUUB

BLUUUUUUUUB

Along comes a clam
With a wide winning grin
And a pearl of advice
For her pal to take in:

"Hey, Mr. Fish,
With your crosstown frown,
Don't you think it's time to
Turn it upside down?"

Says the fish to his friend,
"Nice thought, Ms. Clam.
I hear what you're saying,
But it's just the way I am.

"I'm a *pout-pout* fish
With a *pout-pout* face,
So I spread the dreary-wearies
All over the place."

Along comes a jellyfish.
He floats through the ocean,
His tentacles all trailing
In a gentle locomotion.

"Hey, Mr. Fish,
With your daily scaly scowl,
I wish you wouldn't greet us
With a grimace and a growl."

Says the fish to his friend,
"Mr. Jelly, I agree.
I'd like to be more friendly,
But it isn't up to me.

"I'm a *pout-pout* fish
With a *pout-pout* face,
So I spread the dreary-wearies
All over the place."

Along comes a squid,
Quite a slender squiggly sight.
She is squirmy, she is squelchy,
She is slightly impolite.

"Hey, Mr. Fish,
You kaleidoscope of mope,
How about a smile?
A little joy? A little hope?"

Says the fish to his friend,
"Mrs. Squid, I would try,
But I haven't any choice.
Take a look and you'll see why.

"I'm a *pout-pout* fish
With a *pout-pout* face,
So I spread the dreary-wearies
All over the place."

Along comes an octopus
With eight great arms
Covered on the underside
With tiny sucker charms.

"Hey, Mr. Fish,
Let me tell it to you straight.
Your hulky-bulky sulking
Is an unattractive trait!"

Says the fish to his friend,
"Mr. Eight, my chum,
With a mouth like mine
I am *destined* to be glum.

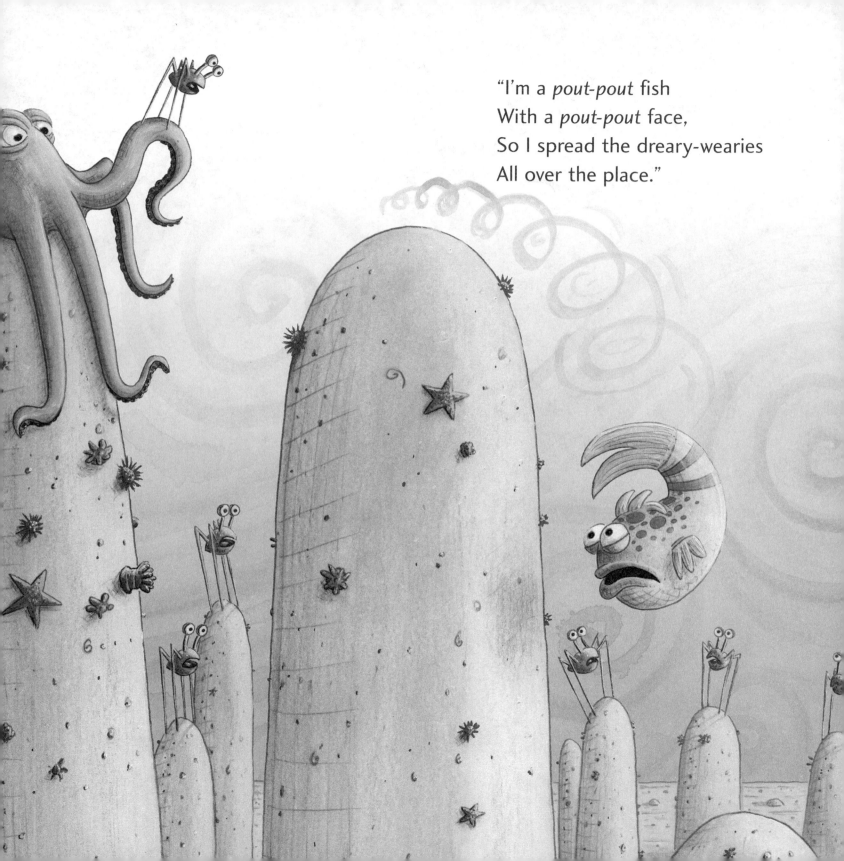

"I'm a *pout-pout* fish
With a *pout-pout* face,
So I spread the dreary-wearies
All over the place."

Now along comes a fish
In a silent silver shimmer.
The gang has never seen before
This bright and brilliant swimmer.

She approaches Mr. Fish,
But instead of saying hey . . .

She plants a kiss upon his pout
And then she swims
Away.

Mr. Fish is most astounded.
Mr. Fish is just aghast.
He is stone-faced like a statue.
Then he blinks, and speaks at last:

"My friends," says Mr. Fish,
"I should have known it all along.
I thought that I was pouty,
But it turns out I was wrong.

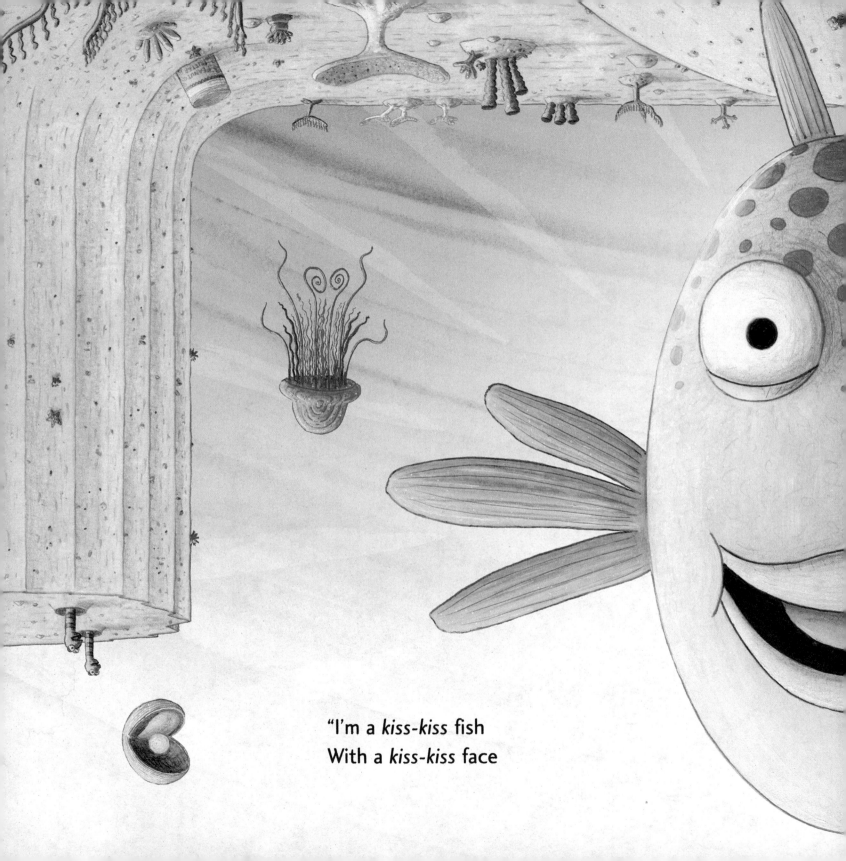

"I'm a *kiss-kiss* fish
With a *kiss-kiss* face

For spreading cheery-cheeries
All over the place!"

So I'll . . .

Smooch

Smooch

Smooch

Smooch